Pick-A-Path® #15

# THE HOT DOG GANG CAPER

by B. B. HILLER and NEIL W. HILLER
illustrated by A. DELANEY

## SCHOLASTIC INC.

New York Toronto London Auckland Sydney Tokyo

ISBN 0-590-33419-0

12 11 10 9 8 7 6 5 4 3 2 1        3        5 6 7 8 9/8 9/9

Printed in the U.S.A.

# Scholastic Books in the Pick-A-Path Series
## How many have you read?

## READ THIS FIRST

Are you ready for some really fantastic adventures?

Start reading on page 1 and keep going until you have to make a choice. Then decide what you want to do and turn to that page.

Keep going until you reach THE END. Then, you can go back and start again. Every path leads to a new story!

It is all up to you!

Swissssh!

Someone has pushed an envelope under your front door. It's got *your* name on it. What could it be?

Maybe you've won a contest! Not likely. Maybe it's an invitation to a party! Or, maybe it's . . .

Oh, stop this! Why don't you just open it?

*Turn to* **page 2.**

Uh oh. It's *not* good news. It's a ransom note!

"The mutt" is a dog named Argyle. The "dough" is the money in that bulging sack that is sitting there on the kitchen table. What *are* you going to do?

*Go on to the next page.*

While you think about it, you run your fingers through the cash. It's a nice feeling. It's a *rich* feeling. You've never *been* rich before — not until you got this sack of money. And you won't *be* rich again if you give in to the dognappers.

*If you'd just as soon keep the money,*
*turn to* **page 4.**

*If you want to stay out of trouble and*
*just pay the dognappers,*
*turn to* **page 33.**

*If you think there's another way out,*
*turn to* **page 7.**

It's not surprising you want to keep the money, because you've got a hunch you'll get Argyle back anyway.

Here's how you got into this mess in the first place. You were riding your bike home with Argyle tagging along, when you ran smack into Derek Portnoy, your next-door neighbor and a *real* bully. Derek grabbed your book bag and heaved it into the garbage dumpster in the alley behind the bank. What a pain he is!

*Go on to the next page.*

Anyway, you had to climb into the    **5**
dumpster to retrieve your book bag.
Your classroom diary was in it and you
sure didn't want to start from September
again! As you were crawling over the
trash, you spotted your book bag! Right
next to it was another bag, a big round
canvas one. You thought it might be
better than your old Smurfs book bag,
but you didn't know how *much* better
until later.

*Turn to* **page 6.**

**6**     You picked up both bags, hopped out of the dumpster and hurried home on your bike. All the way home you had the strange feeling that someone was following you.

Soon after you got home, three things happened: first, you opened the canvas bag and found it *stuffed* with cash. Second, you noticed that Argyle hadn't followed you home. Finally, the ransom note arrived.

Who do you think is behind this?

*If it seems logical that bank robbers followed you home,* turn to **page 44.**

*If you believe Derek Portnoy is not only a bully but a dognapper, too,* turn to **page 27.**

*If you suspect it might be someone in your own family — maybe even wacky old Great Aunt Harriet,* turn to **page 17.**

Of course there's another way out —
you can try to keep the money *and* get
Argyle back. But that will call for some
*very* careful planning. Double-crossing
a double-crosser is tricky business.

Suddenly, the phone starts ringing.
Are you ready for this? You pick it up.

"Police headquarters," you say.

"Hey! Is that *you*?" You recognize the
voice of your very best friend, Terry.

"Boy am I glad to hear your voice. I
thought you were a dognapper!"

"Dognapper?!"

*Turn to* **page 8.**

"Yeah. See, I was carrying a sack of cash to the bank — all the money we made at the school fair. Argyle was with me for protection. Big help he was! Anyway, there was this van that seemed to be following me and when Argyle went to sniff at it, I called to him. 'Here, Argyle, stay away from there,' I said. Well, you know Argyle — "

"Sure I do," says Terry. "Argyle jumped into the van, right?"

"Right. And the van sped off! I was so scared, I just ran home." Then you tell Terry about the ransom note.

*Go on to the next page.*

"You're going to need help." **9**

That's for sure. Terry agrees to come right over.

As soon as you hang up, though, there's another ringing sound. What is it?

*If it's the phone, turn to* **page 21.**

*If it's the doorbell, turn to* **page 10.**

*If it's* both *at the same time, turn to* **page 19.**

You open the door and find a pile of suitcases — a very *big* pile of suitcases. From behind the pile emerges the last person you expected to see — your Great Aunt Harriet.

"Now, what's all this about dognappers?" she asks. "And a bag of money and policemen?"

Golly! How did *she* know???

*If you believe she must be in on it, turn to* **page 12.**

*If you're sure there must be some other explanation, turn to* **page 13.**

Just because everybody knows that Great Aunt Harriet is a little peculiar is no reason to suspect she's one of The Hot Dog Gang. While you were busy on the phone, *she* was busy piling suitcases on the doorstep. Could she have overheard your phone conversation through the open door?

Now, if you want to go on thinking that Great Aunt Harriet is a dognapper, this is . . .

## THE END

(Or, *you can come to your senses and turn to* **page 13** *and find out what really happened. After all, maybe Great Aunt Harriet can help you.*)

"Here, Great Aunt Harriet, let me help you with those suitcases," you say.

"Yes, dear, and while you're doing that, tell me all about the dognapping. I heard you telling your friend the news on the phone. The window's open, you know."

By the time her suitcases are in the guest room, Terry has arrived, full of plans, and the three of you discuss the best way to get Argyle back.

*Turn to* **page 14.**

"Well," suggests Terry, "why don't you just ask the dognappers to meet you someplace to give Argyle back — "

"That's right!" Great Aunt Harriet chimes in. "And *I'll* just order them to do it!"

With friends like this, who needs enemies?

Ring! Ring! That *must* be the dognappers.

Well, who do you trust? You or your helpers?

*If you want to go with Terry and Great Aunt Harriet's plan, turn to* **page 55.**

*If you figure you're better off on your own, turn to* **page 21.**

"Yeah, I've seen these guys. They were around the bank — but how did *you* know?"

"Well, you see that one?" Detective Clue points to the face in the middle. "That's Pug Nation, the ringleader. I've been following him and I saw him stuff something under your door. I knew it *had* to be — "

"The ransom note!" you guess. Detective Clue nods.

"I would have arrested him then, but I still need more evidence. Now here's what we'll do. When the call comes, you agree to meet the gang. By the time you get to the drop-off place, I'll have two squads of undercover police, a back-up SWAT team, and a helicopter 'on station.' We'll get those guys!"

"Gee, Detective Clue," you say, "that would be neat to see — just like something on TV — but I think we can make this a *little* simpler — "

Detective Clue looks at you strangely.

*Turn to* **page 16.**

"Here's what I have in mind." And you tell him your idea. He is surprised by what you tell him about Argyle.

Now you have to decide who you trust. Do you want to go with your plan or with Detective Clue's?

*If you want to try your plan, turn to* **page 35.**

*If you're convinced the police know the best way to handle this kind of thing, turn to* **page 40.**

Your Great Aunt Harriet has a way of getting into strange situations and dragging you in on them. After all, Argyle *is* her dog. She left him with you to dogsit when she left for vacation at the Coconut Cove Country Club. She's going to expect to find him with you — unless she's mixed up in some funny business!

You remember the birthday she gave you a deed to one square inch of a gold field in the Yukon. The next thing you knew, someone from the Canadian embassy was at your door trying to collect back taxes. And once she asked you to take care of her hamsters, Tom and Fred, for the summer. Fred turned out to be Frederika so that by September, you had twenty-seven little furry friends to return to her.

*Turn to* **page 18.**

So, now she's in Coconut Cove and you're in a lot of hot water — wait a minute! Coconut Cove?! You go back and look at the ransom note. It's written on stationery from Coconut Cove Country Club! It can't be coincidence, can it? Why, the only other person you know who's ever *been* to Coconut Cove is Derek, and that was just to visit his Uncle Herc.

*If you guess the answer will be found in Coconut Cove, turn to* **page 42.**

*If you suspect the answer may be closer to home, turn to* **page 27.**

*If it appears that Great Aunt Harriet's gotten you into another mess, turn to* **page 52.**

Thinking Terry must be outside, you open the door wide. But it's not Terry — it's a strange man. He flashes a smile and a badge and introduces himself.

"Hello, I'm Detective Stuart Clue. I've come about the dognapping and I don't want you to answer that phone. Not yet, anyway."

*Turn to* **page 20.**

**20**     He walks into the house. The phone stops ringing. Right away, you suspect something is wrong. In the first place, how could the police *possibly* know about the dognapping? In the second place, *nobody* is named Stu Clue!

"Excuse me, Detective Clue," you say politely. "But, gee, I've never seen a *real* detective before. Could you let me see your badge?"

*If this seems like a phony Clue, turn to* **page 24.**

*If he might be the real thing, turn to* **page 23.**

"Hello?" you say.

"We got your dog," says the gravelly voice at the other end of the phone.

"Oh, I'm so glad you called!" you say, excitedly.

"You are?" says the man.

"Sure! He hasn't bitten you yet, has he?" you ask. "I mean, the vet said we had to be very careful until we get the results of the tests. He probably doesn't really *have* it, but, oh, I hope he hasn't hurt you . . . but if he has, you'll only need fourteen shots and you *probably* won't die."

"What??!"

"Well, that little squirrel was so cute, but kind of mean. Anyway, Argyle doesn't bite *very* much — well, except for the mailman and the exterminator and, well, a couple of other strangers, but *most* of the time he's *pretty* friendly."

*Turn to* **page 22.**

You hear the dognapper drop the phone and yell, "Hey, Lefty, get that mutt outa here. I'll open the door. He's got rabies!"

Then, over the phone, you hear the door open and slam closed. Quietly, you hang up the phone, laughing.

Your dear dog, Argyle, is on his way home.

Now *that's* how you double-cross a double-crosser!

**THE END**

Detective Clue hands you the wallet. **23**
It sure *looks* like the real thing. You
give it back to him.

"Thanks. Now, here's something *else*
I'd like to show you." From another
pocket, he pulls a "Wanted" poster. It
looks like this:

So *this* is The Hot Dog Gang! You
look closely at the pictures. Is there
something familiar about those faces?

*If you've seen them before,*
*turn to* **page 15.**

*If they seem totally strange to you,*
*turn to* **page 39.**

One look at the badge and you know this man's an imposter. The badge looks like it came from a box of Cracker Jacks! He must be one of the dognappers! You had better not let him know that *you* know he's a phony. That would be real trouble for you. Casually, you return the badge to him.

"Okay," he says. "Now, you give *me* the money for the dognappers and we'll get those sneaky guys behind bars! See? I have my deputies outside ready to make the arrests." You look through the window to see the other two dognappers and the van.

Before you can reply, the doorbell rings. It's Terry.

"Come on in," you say, warmly. "Hey, Detective Clue, I want you to meet my best friend, Terry."

*Go on to the next page.*

There's no stopping Terry's laughter at the man's name.

"Okay, Terry, knock off the fun and games," you say. "We have some serious business to take care of. Detective Clue and I were talking about the ransom money. He wants to hold it until The Hot Dog Gang calls. So why don't you go get the ransom money from your house where you stashed it, and we'll give it to Detective Clue."

"But how could I . . . I mean . . ."

"That's okay, Terry." You give him a secret wink. "We can trust this man. He's a police officer. So, you go home and get the money and bring the whole bunch back here for the *police*. I think The Hot Dog Gang must be nearby, too, so it won't be long now, until my dog *Fergus* is home again."

*Turn to* **page 26.**

The light dawns.

"Oh, sure, I remember where the money is. I put it right by the *phone*. Yeah, well, I'll be right back with it."

Terry leaves. Now you must wait.

But you don't have to wait long. Within minutes the place is completely surrounded by *real* police — the ones Terry called on the phone.

Quickly, they round up the guys in the van and arrest the phony Detective Clue.

Argyle is safe in the van. The money is safe in your home. You and Terry become heroes and get your pictures in the paper.

**THE END**

You're sure Derek must be the dognapper. He had you rummage through
the garbage just so he could steal Argyle.
Very funny.

However, there's the matter of the
money. You decide to look at that stuff
again — under a good light. After just a
few seconds, you can tell it's phony as
can be.

*Turn to* **page 28.**

Now you wonder how you can get back at Derek. Slowly, a plan forms in your mind. You only have to wait for the call from Derek.

Soon it comes.

"This is The Hot Dog Gang," a gruff but familiar voice rasps.

"Come off it, Derek." Derek, however, won't give in easily.

"Who's Derek? This is The Hot Dog — "

"Derek, I give up. You've had your laugh, but I'm wise to you now."

Derek gives in.

*Go on to the next page.*

"Listen, why don't you just send Argyle home? I'm sure you want this money back," you say.

"Nah. You can have it."

You pause.

"*All* of it?"

"Sure. It's just . . . What do you mean *all* of it?"

"Say, Derek," you begin, as calmly as you know how. "Did you look at all the bills you stuffed in the bag?"

"No. It's just photocopied money," Derek hesitates, then continues, "isn't it?"

You ignore the question.

"Good-bye, Derek." You hang up. The hook is baited.

From under your bed, you get the box where you've been stashing most of your allowance. Then the phone rings again.

"Hi, it's Derek. I've let Argyle go, okay? Now, about that money. . . ."

The fish has taken the bait.

*Go to* **page 30.**

**30**     "I have to go now," you say. "I have an appointment at the bank with Mr. Jones, the manager. Good-bye." Again, you hang up quickly.

Before you go into the bank, you throw the counterfeit money into the dumpster behind the building, and put your saved-up allowance into the canvas sack.

As you enter the bank and walk up to Mr. Jones's desk, his phone rings.

"This is Mr. Jones. Can I help you?" You hold your breath until he speaks again.

"Yes, Derek. Sure. Well, in fact your friend is here with me now."

The fish is *definitely* hooked.

"Well, Derek, I know you understand that I can't discuss your friend's account with you — " Mr. Jones pauses to listen as he looks through the bag.

*Go to* **page 32**.

"No, Derek," he continues. "Of course it's not counterfeit money in the canvas bag. It's bona fide American dollars."

There's another pause. You're pretty sure you know what Derek is asking now. Mr. Jones's answer proves you are right. "Well, Derek, the idea of 'a lot' of money is relative. Banks have *millions*. But, yes, I'd say this is, indeed, a large deposit."

You bet it is! Twenty-seven dollars and thirteen cents. It took you a long time to save that much money!

Now your job is done. Argyle is home; you've finally put your allowance money in the bank; and Derek, the fish, has been landed. This is . . .

## THE END

That's a strange attitude for someone who doesn't want trouble! It seems more like you're looking for it! Don't you know you can't trust a crook?

Still, when the phone call comes, you agree to pay up. That's the way you are. You'll do anything to save a little dog — even give up the money you just won for being the town Frisbee champion.

And it's not even *your* little dog. In fact, it's your neighbor's obnoxious, noisy, yappy little dog. Why did you decide to fork over all that beautiful cash? Now you're stuck. Maybe the dog will be so grateful, he'll start behaving . . . maybe.

*Turn to* **page 34.**

You follow the dognappers' instructions to the word and pretty soon Argyle has returned home and they've got the cash. Know what you get for your trouble?

Woof, woof, arf, grrrrr, ruff, yap, yap, yap! All night long.

Boy, this is . . .

## THE END

When the phone call comes, the gravelly voice identifies himself as Pug Nation of The Hot Dog Gang. He gives you instructions to meet him in the warehouse behind the bank. You agree, but first, you say, "Let me talk to Argyle. I have to know he's okay."

"Sure, kid."

Soon you hear his familiar panting.

"Hi, Argyle. Speak!" Argyle is silent.

"Good boy. Now, I want you to be a good doggie, okay? I don't want you to bite that man's ankle when I give him a bag, okay? Now, hush, boy." Argyle barks.

Pug Nation takes the phone. "Okay, kid. See you at the warehouse in fifteen minutes." He hangs up.

You wink at Detective Clue who was listening on the extension phone.

*Go to* **page 37.**

The stage is set.

A little while later you enter the warehouse, carrying the money bag. From a shadow emerges the dognapper, Pug Nation. Argyle is on a leash. You smile when you see him.

"Heel, Argyle!" you say, and watch your dog begin to run around Nation, tangling his legs in the leash. Once, twice, three times. Nation is taken by surprise.

"Sorry, Mr. Nation. Here's the money." You hand him the bag. Argyle promptly starts nipping at the man's ankles, then he begins to bite in earnest.

"Don't growl!"

"Grrrrrrr!" Boy, it's neat that Argyle is completely reliable. He does the *exact* opposite of what anyone says — every time!

*Go to* **page 38.**

Within seconds, Detective Clue has Nation completely tied up. His officers have captured Nation's henchmen. It's over!

Argyle is ready to return home, and the money is recovered. For his part, Detective Clue is relishing the idea of grilling The Hot Dog Gang before they are rolled to jail. There won't be any picnic for these Hot Dogs!

**THE END**

"Well," says Detective Clue, "don't worry if you haven't seen them. Trust me — you *will* see them — behind bars!"

Detective Clue, it seems, has been tracking these guys for a long time, and they were last seen snooping around your house. *That's* how he guessed about the dognapping.

"Listen," he tells you. "When they call, you agree to follow their orders to the letter. If you tell us their plan, we'll find a way to get the dog *and* the money."

That sounds to you like quite a promise from someone who's been unsuccessfully tracking this bunch for more than a year. But he probably knows best — maybe.

*Turn to* **page 40.**

Soon, the call comes. You are to put the bag of cash in the dumpster behind the bank. That's strange, but you agree to do it.

As soon as you tell Detective Clue, he sends two squadrons of police to watch the dumpster. At the agreed time, you walk past the dumpster and heave the bag in.

For four hours, you see absolutely nothing happen at the dumpster. Finally, a police officer looks carefully into the dumpster and sees . . .

*Go on to the next page.*

Quickly, the police move the dumpster to find a hole in the bottom of it
which leads to an open manhole under-
neath. You and the police have been
tricked by The Hot Dog Gang! Good-
bye, money!

The good news is that at least the gang
holds up *their* end of the deal. A little
while later a tired but healthy Argyle
trots back up the street and into your
arms.

**THE END**

You're on your way upstairs to get your toothbrush and bathing suit, when the phone rings. You pick it up.

"You listening, kid? Okay, how about you put our money back where you got it from *now*. That is, if you ever want to see this mutt again. . . ."

Forget the toothbrush! You've got to get that money to the dumpster! The alley is deserted as you toss the money bag into the dumpster.

But when you get home again, you find a police squad car and a fire engine in front of the house. People seem to be lurking behind bushes and you hear the drone of a helicopter above.

What have you done???

*Maybe it's time to face the music.*
*Turn to* **page 45.**

*But if you think there's no time like the present to get to Coconut Cove,*
*turn to* **page 46.**

Sure, who else but robbers would put money in a dumpster behind the bank? They must have been interrupted in the middle of a robbery.

If it's bank robbers, there's no doubt about it — you'll need the police in on it. You call them, and quickly their crack inspector, Detective Clue, arrives on the scene. He wisely advises you to follow the dognappers' orders to the letter.

"I've worked on lots of these cases. You're always better off at least appearing to go along with them."

You have to agree that makes sense. But the question is, who is going to run this show — you or the police?

*You have an idea of your own. If you want to go with your plan, turn to **page 35**.*

*If you agree to use Detective Clue's plan, turn to **page 40**.*

You ride your bike up to your house and go up to the man waiting on your doorstep. He introduces himself as Detective Clue, shows you his badge, and demands: "*What* have you done with the money? We lost your trail when you left by the back door!"

"Well, sir — " you begin and tell all, hoping for the best.

The best is *not* what you get. Because, you see, it turns out that Argyle never *was* dognapped! He'd been accidentally locked in the cellar the whole time. And for *that* you turned over forty-seven years worth of allowance to some bank robbers!

At least you got Argyle back — but then he'd never been gone!

Boy, this is . . .

**THE END**

**46**

The next morning, you climb off the train at Coconut Cove. It's a relief to be there because hiding in a baggage car is *no* way to travel!

The big surprise is that Great Aunt Harriet is *waiting* for you at the station!

"Oh, dear!" she says, hugging you. "Your mother called. She was frantic with worry, but at least you left that note —"

Note? What note!

*Go on to the next page.**Go on to the next page.*

" — saying 'I'm going to Coconut Cove,'" Great Aunt Harriet continued. "But why did you write it with cut-up pieces of newspaper? Well, here you are and let's call home to say you're okay."

Boy, this is getting crazy now! Whoever *took* the dog must have left the note — but who?

You decide to tell Great Aunt Harriet everything that's happened. As you talk, though, you realize she's not listening. All her attention is focused on a man she sees on the boardwalk — a friend, apparently.

*Turn to* **page 49.**

"My dear," she says to you, "I'm going to introduce you to a friend of mine — a *very important* friend, understand?" Sure you understand. He must be rich. "Now, he is something of a practical joker, so don't mind." Okay, you think. Your story can wait.

You shake hands with Hercules Portnoy, as you are introduced, only to find one of those dumb buzzer things vibrating in your palm. Some joke. Mr. Portnoy laughs uncontrollably. You and Great Aunt Harriet smile politely.

"Oh, Herc," she says. "You and your jokes — "

Herc, you think. That's an odd name. Herc. Hmmm. Wait a minute! This is Derek's "Uncle Herc!" He's a practical joker, too, just like Derek. You realize that you've finally gotten hold of the thread that will unravel this mystery.

*Turn to* **page 50.**

"Uh, Mr. Portnoy," you say, "you and Derek sure were pulling a fast one on me with the dognapping scheme!" With a start, Uncle Herc realizes who you are.

"Oh, ho, ho, ho, ho! How did you like that trick? We thought you'd think that was funny." Again, he starts laughing. You know he's the one who enjoys his own jokes the most. He may be the only one who does.

". . . And the notes!" he continues, between snorts. "And how about the counterfeit money?" Ha ha. So funny you forget to laugh. Well, that's that. Now everything is explained. No, not everything. What about the police and firemen at your house?

*Go on to the next page.*

You get the answer to that when you call home. Derek, it seems, was also playing practical jokes on the town emergency teams. Boy, were they mad! Derek has been grounded for a month. That's okay, though, because now he's dogsitting for Argyle while you have a fantastic vacation in Coconut Cove!

## THE END

What's wacky Great Aunt Harriet gotten you into this time? When you call Coconut Cove, you find that she's left. Something's fishy. Next, you call your mother at her office and tell her about the note.

Your mother laughs. "It must be one of Aunt Harriet's little jokes," she says. "I just talked to her — she's back and she just picked Argyle up at our house."

And left a phony ransom note, you think. Some joke.

*Go on to the next page.*

Sweet revenge enters your mind. You call Great Aunt Harriet at home and try to sound as grown-up as possible.

"Hello," you say. "This is Major Duguet of the Royal Canadian Mounted Police. We've got a youngster here who claims to be chasing dognappers to recover your dog. But a check of our records reveals that he is wanted for back taxes in the Yukon Territory — "

"Oh, no, Major!"

"Yes, Ma'am. So before we put the kid in the slammer — "

*Turn to* **page 54.**

— and forget about him — "

"Oh, no, Major!"

"Yes, Ma'am. We wanted to check — "

"Oh, no, Major!"

How loyal she is to you, you think. Well, that's enough of that. You interrupt her.

"Great Aunt Harriet — "

"Yes, Major?"

"No, Great Aunt Harriet, it's *me*!" Finally, she realizes the joke's on her and it's a good one. You both laugh a little about the dognapping, too.

But what about the sack of cash? Great Aunt Harriet, it seems, knows nothing about it and had nothing to do with it. Now what?

You call the police to find they know nothing about it either. There were no robberies, and no one reported losing a bundle of bucks. Know what that means? That means that you turn it over to the police and wait. And if, after a year, nobody else claims the cash, it's yours. Boy, that would be . . .

**THE END**

Great Aunt Harriet, you see, is sort of a take-charge person. Nobody has ever been able to say *no* to her. You know that the dognappers won't be able to, either.

When the phone rings, she answers it. Before the dognapper can start giving orders, Great Aunt Harriet jumps in with both feet.

"Now, listen to me, young man," she says. "I want you and all your little ruffian friends to bring that doggie right back where he belongs. If you insist on getting paid for your trouble, I guess that would be understandable. Just have Argyle at the Kennel Club Championship Show at the Sports Arena this afternoon at four o'clock sharp. We'll meet you between the Chow Chows and the Lhasa Apsos. That's by Ring A3. The money will be in a nylon backpack."

She hangs up.

*Turn to* **page 56.**

That gives you just enough time to call your friends Alison, Charlie, and the whole gang to help. By the time four o'clock rolls around, the stage is set.

You enter the dog show, wearing your nylon backpack. You are followed by twenty classmates, all wearing nylon backpacks. You are carrying Aunt Harriet's poodle, Fifi. Each of your classmates is also carrying a dog. Aunt Harriet is in front of this parade, holding a clipboard and wearing two whistles, a normal one and a dog whistle.

You have a kid standing guard at each entrance to the show, ready to alert the rest of the team the moment the dognappers arrive with Argyle.

Soon, very soon, Alison gives the high sign. As the dognappers make their way to Ring A3, Aunt Harriet blows the dog whistle. All the dogs begin barking hysterically. Argyle springs out of the arms of the dognapper and runs around frantically, looking for the person who blew the dog whistle.

*Turn to* **page 58.**

All the other dogs, carried by your friends, jump down, too. These dognappers are not a dumb bunch — not at all. They know they've been had, but good. Quickly, they begin the search for the nylon backpack. Within seconds, they've found it. So they think. Wrong kid. There's another. Wrong again. Not only have they been had, but they've *really* been had. They decide to beat it.

You've got your dog and the money. The police, alerted by Great Aunt Harriet, are waiting for the dognappers outside — good old Great Aunt Harriet told them to be there. See, *nobody* ever says *no* to her. Only *you* know that her bark is worse than her bite. Most of the time.

**THE END**